3

It's My Party!

A Book About Sharing

by Justin Spelvin   illustrated by Larissa Marantz and Katharine DiPaolo

SIMON SPOTLIGHT/NICK JR.
New York   London   Toronto   Sydney

KN

Based on the TV series *LazyTown*™ as seen on Nick Jr.®

SIMON SPOTLIGHT
An imprint of Simon & Schuster Children's Publishing Division
1230 Avenue of the Americas, New York, New York 10020
LazyTown © & ™ 2006 LazyTown Entertainment. Copyright © 2006 LazyTown Entertainment. All rights reserved.
All related titles, logos, and characters are trademarks of LazyTown Entertainment.
NICK JR. and all related titles, logos, and characters are registered trademarks of
Viacom International Inc.
Created by Magnús Scheving.
All rights reserved, including the right of reproduction in whole or in part in any form.
SIMON SPOTLIGHT and colophon are registered trademarks of Simon & Schuster, Inc.
Manufactured in the United States of America
First Edition
2 4 6 8 10 9 7 5 3 1
ISBN-13: 978-1-4169-1536-2
ISBN-10: 1-4169-1536-2

It was a bright, sunny LazyTown morning. Stingy woke up even happier than usual.

It was his birthday.

"How perfect!" said Stingy. "It's *my* birthday. A day that's all *mine*!"

He jumped out of bed and wondered what presents he would get.

Stephanie and the gang were already hard at work decorating the town square. They were planning a surprise party for Stingy! There would be games, lots of presents, and even boxcar races!

"This is going to be the best birthday ever!" Stephanie said as she finished painting a huge banner.

"It'll be totally far out," added Pixel as he hung up the right side of the banner.

"Now that's what I call teamwork!" Sportacus said as he hung up the left side.

Ziggy was in charge of the food.

Stephanie helped Trixie set up Stingy's favorite game, Pin the Dollar on the Piggy.

Pixel and Sportacus made sure the boxcars were rolling.

And Mayor Meanswell and Bessie Busybody lined up all the presents.

"I'll be right back," said Sportacus, dashing away. "I'm going to get my special energy cake!"

But just then the birthday boy arrived!
"Surprise!" everyone cheered.
"How did you know it was my birthday?" Stingy asked.

"What are you talking about?" said Trixie. "You put an ad in the paper."

Everyone laughed. Then Bessie put on some music and the party started.

But one person was not dancing, laughing, playing games, or racing boxcars. And that same person couldn't take a nap either. It was Robbie Rotten.

"How am I supposed to sleep away the day with all that NOISE?" he grumbled. "If only there was a way to break up this party. . . ."

Just then Robbie had a very rotten idea. He started looking for a disguise.

Everyone was enjoying Stingy's party when an unexpected visitor arrived.

"Birthday mail!" Robbie said, disguising his voice.

"That's *mine*!" said Stingy. "It's *my* birthday, after all."

Stingy looked around. The mailman was right! If he wanted to play a game or race or have a snack, he would have to wait his turn. He would have to *share*. How could it be *his* party if he had to *share* everything?

Just then Bessie called out, "Time for presents!"

But Stingy had seen enough.

"That's *mine*!" Stingy shouted, grabbing a present.
The party got very quiet.
"The games are *mine*. The cars are *mine*. The food is *mine*," Stingy continued. "This whole party is *mine*. It's *my* birthday, *not* yours!" he yelled.

"But Stingy," Stephanie explained, "we wanted you to have a great party."

"I *will*," Stingy answered, "when I don't have to share any of it. Good-bye."

Stingy's friends slowly left the party.

"I guess we can go to my house," Pixel said quietly.

"It's finally *my* party!" Stingy shouted. He tore open all his presents. "Yahoo!" he yelled. "I got everything I wanted!"

But no one was there to admire his presents.

He pinned dollar after dollar on the Piggy. "I win again!" he cheered.

But no one was there to cheer back.

Stingy rushed over to a boxcar and jumped in. "I can race myself!" he announced.

But there was no one there to push.

Stingy wasn't getting very far. He was starting to think that a party without his friends wasn't much fun at all.

Just then Sportacus ran in. "Sorry I'm late!" he said. "Hey, where did everyone go?"

Sportacus listened while Stingy told him what had happened.

"Did telling everyone to leave make you happy?" Sportacus asked. Stingy shook his head.

"I know where we need to go," said Sportacus. "Let's roll."

"Surprise!" shouted Sportacus. He and Stingy burst into Pixel's house. The gang cheered up as soon as they saw Stingy.

"We're sorry you didn't like your party," said Stephanie.

"No, *I'm* sorry," said Stingy. "A party isn't a party if you can't share it with your friends."

"Let's have the party right here!" said Pixel. Everyone agreed.

"We're going to need . . . ," Sportacus began as he opened the box, "my famous energy cake!"

"Blow out the candles on your cake, Stingy," said Stephanie.

"I have a better idea," said Stingy. "Let's all blow them out together."

So together they blew out the birthday candles. It was the start of the best party Stingy had ever had. Everyone was happy.

Well, almost everyone.